Willow's Smile

To my goddaughter, Jamie, and my godson, Matthew, with smiles! — L.B.

To my mum, for always being there for me — T.H.

Kids Can Press acknowledges the financial support of the Government of Ontario, through the Ontario Media Development Corporation's Ontario Book Initiative; the Ontario Arts Council; the Canada Council for the Arts; and the Government of Canada, through the CBF, for our publishing activity.

Published in Canada by
Kids Can Press Ltd.
25 Dockside Drive
Toronto, ON M5A 0B5

Published in the U.S. by
Kids Can Press Ltd.
2250 Military Road
Tonawanda, NY 14150

www.kidscanpress.com

Kids Can Press is a Corus™ Entertainment company

The artwork in this book was rendered in Photoshop.
The text is set in Univers 45 and Bodoni.

Edited by Debbie Rogosin
Designed by Karen Powers

This book is smyth sewn casebound.
Manufactured in Shenzhen, Guang Dong, P.R. China, in 9/2015 by Printplus Limited.

CM 16 0 9 8 7 6 5 4 3 2 1

Library and Archives Canada Cataloguing in Publication

Button, Lana, 1968–, author

Willow's smile / written by Lana Button ; illustrated by Tania Howells.

(Willow)
ISBN 978-1-77138-549-7 (bound)

I. Howells, Tania, illustrator II. Title.

PS8603.U87W53 2016 jC813'.6 C2015-903271-7

Willow's Smile

Written by Lana Button Illustrated by Tania Howells

KIDS CAN PRESS

Sometimes Willow smiled without even trying.

But sometimes, when she wished she could, and knew she should, her smile slipped straight off her face.

It seemed like Willow *wouldn't.*
But sometimes, she just *couldn't.*

At school, Mrs. Post made an announcement. "Boys and girls, tomorrow is Picture Day."

"OOOOOOH!" squealed Kristabelle. "*I'm* going to wear my fanciest things so I look *picture perfect*!"

"I'll wear something special, too!" Tianna said excitedly.

"Just bring your smile," said Mrs. Post.

As they headed out the door, everyone flashed a Picture Day smile.

Everyone but Willow.

At home, Willow studied her smile.

Did it look picture perfect when she was dressed like this?

Or this?

Or this?

She decided her smile came out best like this.

But Willow was worried. What if she couldn't smile on Picture Day?

flour
sugar

"I'm sure your picture will be perfect,"
Willow's dad said the next morning as
he added ribbons to her hair.

While he pulled and tugged at Willow's ribbons,
she pulled and tugged her cheeks into practice smiles.

Willow's class was bubbling with Picture Day excitement.

Juan patted his spiky hair.

Jane jangled an armful of bracelets.

And Kristabelle did a twirl. "Look at my shiny shoes!"

But Willow noticed that not everyone looked happy.

"I forgot about Picture Day," Tianna said sadly. "I wanted to wear something special."

Willow wondered if a ribbon might make Tianna feel better.

It did.

As Tianna's tears disappeared, Willow found her smile.

It spread all by itself, right across her face …

... until Mrs. Post flicked the lights. "Line up, boys and girls. It's our turn for pictures."

With every step Willow took,
her smile slipped
further down her face.

The gym doors opened. As soon as Willow saw the big lights and the camera with its bright flash, she hid behind her hands. Her smile was gone for good.

How could she have her picture taken now?

"Willow," said Mrs. Post, guiding her out of line. "Our photographer, Mr. Corbett, could use some help."

"Hooray, my assistant is here!" said Mr. Corbett. He handed Willow a rubber chicken. "When I give a wave, could you please wiggle him in the air?"

It sounded very silly. But Willow was so relieved that she wouldn't have to smile for this job, she took the chicken. She even gave it a little practice wiggle.

"Teeeeeerrrrific!!" said Mr. Corbett. "And here's our first customer!"

Julian was wearing a fancy shirt, a new tie — and a big frown.

"Hop right onto that stool, sir. And sit up reeeeeeally tall."

Mr. Corbett ducked behind his camera and asked Willow, "Who is this young man?"

"Julian," Willow said softly.

Mr. Corbett's head popped up. "Did you say his name is *Mr. Stinky Feet*?!?!" He waved his hand.

With a little giggle, Willow wiggled the chicken in the air.

Julian's frown disappeared!

He hopped off the stool and gave Mr. Corbett a high five!

When Mr. Corbett said, "Look over here, Miss Curly Sue," Kristabelle struck a confident pose.

But Tianna climbed onto the stool looking quite uncertain. Then she heard Mr. Corbett say, "Well, hello there, Fancy Nancy!" and she saw Willow dancing the rubber chicken.

One by one, Willow helped her friends find their own special smiles. And Willow watched as, one by one, they each gave Mr. Corbett a proud high five.

Mr. Corbett turned to Willow. "Okay, Suzie Q, you're my last customer. Are you ready?"

Willow thought about how her friends had looked picture perfect, each in their own way.

And that's when she decided that *her* way of looking picture perfect didn't have to include a smile.

Willow climbed onto the stool.

She placed her hands in her lap, took a brave breath and sat up nice and tall.

She did it!

And then Willow noticed ...

… that all of her friends were standing behind Mr. Corbett!

They were waving and calling out the silliest names!

Hey, Mrs. Tickle Toes!

Hi, Silly Billy!!

Over here, Sparkle Sandwich!!

Willow couldn't help it.

She smiled!

"Great job, Missy Lou," said Mr. Corbett.

Willow gave him a big high five.

Then Mr. Corbett grouped the whole class together.

And on the count of three, everyone cheered. “STINKY FEET!!!”